Love
Penny, Sara
&
Aunt Kathy

Read Me a Story

hinkler

Published by Hinkler Books Pty Ltd
45–55 Fairchild Street
Heatherton Victoria 3202 Australia
www.hinkler.com.au

hinkler

© Hinkler Books Pty Ltd 2011, 2013

Cover Design: Hinkler Design Studio and Peter Tovey
Cover Illustration: Janet Samuel
Internal Design: Hinkler Design Studio and Steve Williams
Illustrations: Janet Samuel, Anton Petrov, Melissa Webb,
Andrew Hopgood, Gerad Taylor, Geoff Cook,
Bill Wood, Marten Coombe, Brijbasi Art Press Ltd
Prepress: Graphic Print Group

ISBN: 978 1 7435 2802 0

Printed and bound in China

Contents

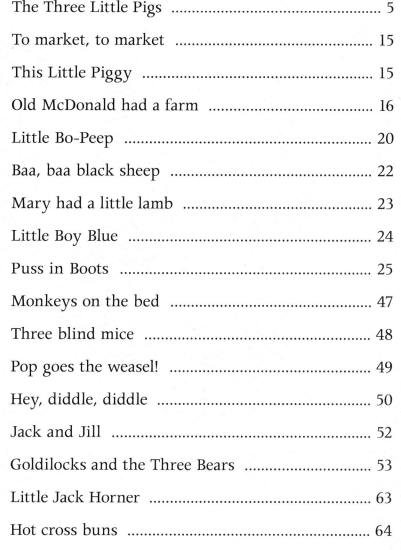

Contents

The Three Little Pigs

Once upon a time there lived a mother sow with her Three Little Pigs. As she did not have enough money to look after them she sent them out into the world to seek their fortunes.

As he was walking down the road, the First Little Pig met a man carrying a bundle of straw. 'Please, sir, give me that straw so I can build a house with it.'

The man gave the straw to the First Little Pig, who went and built a house with it.

As he was walking down the road, the Second Little Pig met a man carrying a bundle of sticks. 'Please, sir, give me those sticks so I can build a house with them.'

The man gave the sticks to the Second Little Pig, who went and built a house with them.

As he was walking down the road, the Third Little Pig met a man carrying a pile of bricks. 'Please, sir, give me those bricks so I can build a house with them.'

The man gave the bricks to the Third Little Pig, who went and built a house with them.

The Three Little Pigs lived happily until one day when a big bad Wolf came to the house of straw. The Wolf knocked at the door of the house made of straw and said, 'Little Pig, Little Pig, let me come in!'

The First Little Pig replied, 'No, not by the hair of my chinny chin chin!'

'Then I'll huff and I'll puff and I'll blow your house in!' cried the Wolf.

So the big bad Wolf huffed and he puffed and he blew down the house of straw. The First Little Pig ran as fast as he could to his brother's house of sticks.

Presently the big bad Wolf came to the house of sticks. The Wolf knocked at the door of the house made of sticks and said, 'Little Pig, Little Pig, let me come in!'

The First Little Pig and the Second Little Pig replied, 'No, not by the hair of my chinny chin chin!'

'Then I'll huff and I'll puff and I'll blow your house in!' cried the Wolf.

So the big bad Wolf huffed and he puffed and he huffed and he puffed and he blew down the house of sticks. The First Little Pig and the Second Little Pig ran as fast as they could to their brother's house of bricks.

Presently the big bad Wolf came to the house of bricks. The Wolf
knocked at the door of the house made of bricks and said, 'Little Pig,
Little Pig, let me come in!'

The First Little Pig and the Second Little Pig and the Third Little Pig
replied, 'No, not by the hair of my chinny chin chin!'

'Then I'll huff and I'll puff and I'll blow your house in!' cried the Wolf.

So the big bad Wolf huffed and he puffed and he huffed and he puffed
and he huffed and he puffed but he could not blow down the house of bricks.

When the Wolf realised that he could not blow down the house of bricks with his huffing and puffing, he said, 'Little Pig, I know where there is a nice field of juicy, tasty turnips.'

'Where?' asked the Third Little Pig.

'In Farmer Brown's field,' replied the Wolf. 'I will call for you at six o'clock tomorrow morning and we will go together to get some for our dinner.'

The next morning the clever Third Little Pig got up at five o'clock and went by himself to get the turnips. 'Are you ready to get some turnips?' asked the Wolf, when he arrived at the Pig's house at six o'clock.

'Ready? I have already been and come back with a nice potful for my dinner!' replied the Third Little Pig.

The Wolf was very angry. He said, 'Little Pig, I know where there is a nice apple tree.'

'Where?' asked the Third Little Pig.

'In Farmer Smith's orchard,' replied the Wolf. 'I will call for you at five o'clock tomorrow morning, and we will go together to get some juicy, tasty apples.'

However, the clever Third Little Pig got up at four o'clock and went to the apple tree. As he had further to go he was still up the tree picking apples when he saw the angry Wolf coming.

'Little Pig come down and tell me if they are nice apples,' called the Wolf.

'They're very nice,' replied the Third Little Pig. 'Here, let me throw you one.' And he threw an apple so far that the Wolf had to go a long way to pick it up and the Little Pig was able to jump down and run home.

The next day the Wolf came and said to the Third Little Pig, 'Little Pig, there is a fair in town. Will you go with me at three o'clock this afternoon?'

'Very well,' said the Third Little Pig.

The Third Little Pig went off earlier to the fair and had a lovely time. He bought a butter churn and was heading home when he saw the Wolf coming. In a panic, he crawled inside the butter churn to hide and it fell over. Down the hill it rolled. When he saw the churn rolling towards him, the Wolf ran away in fright.

The Wolf went to the Third Little Pig's house and told him how he'd been frightened by a great round thing rolling down the hill towards him.

'Dear me, I hid inside the butter churn when I saw you coming and it rolled down the hill. I'm sorry I frightened you,' said the Third Little Pig.

The Wolf grew angry and swore that he would come down the chimney and eat up the First Little Pig and the Second Little Pig and the Third Little Pig. But while he was climbing on to the roof, the Third Little Pig made a blazing fire and put a big pot of water on to boil. As the Wolf was climbing down the chimney the Third Little Pig took off the lid and – splash! – the Wolf fell into the scalding water.

The Wolf howled and leapt so high that he jumped right out of the chimney. He ran off down the road as fast as he could. The Three Little Pigs lived happily ever after in the house of bricks and never saw the big bad Wolf again.

TO MARKET, TO MARKET

To market, to market, to buy a fat pig,
Home again, home again, jiggety-jig;
To market, to market, to buy a fat hog,
Home again, home again, jiggety-jog.
To market, to market, to buy a plum bun;
Home again, home again, market is done.

THIS LITTLE PIGGY

This little piggy went to market,
This little piggy stayed at home;
This little piggy had roast beef,
This little piggy had none;
And this little piggy cried,
'Wee-wee-wee,'
All the way home.

OLD MCDONALD HAD A FARM

Old McDonald had a farm,
E-I-E-I-O!
And on that farm he had a cow,
E-I-E-I-O!
With a moo-moo here,
  and a moo-moo there,
Here a moo, there a moo,
Everywhere a moo-moo!
Old McDonald had a farm,
E-I-E-I-O!

Old McDonald had a farm,
E-I-E-I-O!
And on that farm he had a pig,
E-I-E-I-O!
With an oink-oink here,
    and an oink-oink there,
Here an oink, there an oink,
Everywhere an oink-oink!
Old McDonald had a farm,
E-I-E-I-O!

Old McDonald had a farm,
E-I-E-I-O!
And on that farm he had a horse,
E-I-E-I-O!
With a neigh-neigh here,
    and a neigh-neigh there,
Here a neigh, there a neigh,
Everywhere a neigh-neigh!
Old McDonald had a farm,
E-I-E-I-O!

Old McDonald had a farm,
E-I-E-I-O!
And on that farm he had some sheep,
E-I-E-I-O!
With a baa-baa here,
    and a baa-baa there,
Here a baa, there a baa,
Everywhere a baa-baa!
Old McDonald had a farm,
E-I-E-I-O!

Old McDonald had a farm,
E-I-E-I-O!
And on that farm he had a duck,
E-I-E-I-O!
With a quack-quack here,
    and a quack-quack there,
Here a quack, there a quack,
Everywhere a quack-quack!
Old McDonald had a farm,
E-I-E-I-O!

Old McDonald had a farm,
E-I-E-I-O!
And on that farm he had a dog,
E-I-E-I-O!
With a woof-woof here,
    and a woof-woof there,
Here a woof, there a woof,
Everywhere a woof-woof!
Old McDonald had a farm,
E-I-E-I-O!

LITTLE BO-PEEP

Little Bo-Peep has lost her sheep,
And can't tell where to find them;
Leave them alone, and they'll come home,
And bring their tails behind them.

Little Bo-Peep fell fast asleep,
And dreamed she heard them bleating;
But when she awoke she found it a joke,
For they were still a-fleeting.

Then up she took her little crook,
Determined for to find them;
She found them indeed, but it made her heart bleed,
For they'd left their tails behind them.

It happened one day, as Bo-Peep did stray
Into a meadow hard by,
There she spied their tails side by side,
All hung on a tree to dry.

She heaved a sigh, and wiped her eye,
And over the hillocks went rambling,
And tried what she could,
    as a shepherdess should,
To tack each again to its lambkin.

BAA, BAA, BLACK SHEEP

Baa, baa, black sheep,
Have you any wool?
Yes, sir, yes, sir,
Three bags full;
One for the master,
And one for the dame,
And one for the little boy
Who lives down the lane.

MARY HAD A LITTLE LAMB

$\mathcal{M}$ary had a little lamb,
Its fleece was white as snow;
And everywhere that Mary went
The lamb was sure to go.

It followed her to school one day,
Which was against the rule;
It made the children laugh and play
To see a lamb at school.

And so the teacher turned it out,
But still it lingered near,
And waited patiently about
Till Mary did appear.

'What makes the lamb love Mary so?'
The eager children cry;
'Why, Mary loves the lamb, you know,'
The teacher did reply.

LITTLE BOY BLUE

Little Boy Blue,
Come blow your horn,
The sheep's in the meadow,
The cow's in the corn.

Where is the boy
Who looks after the sheep?
He's under the haystack,
Fast asleep.

Will you wake him?
No, not I,
For if I do,
He's sure to cry.

Puss in Boots

Once upon a time, there was an old miller who died, leaving nothing for his three sons apart from his mill, his donkey and his cat.

The three sons decided to split this poor property between themselves. The eldest son took the mill, the second son took the donkey and the youngest son received nothing but the cat.

Understandably, the youngest son was quite disappointed that his share was so poor. 'My brothers may make a handsome enough living if they combine their shares together,' said the youngest son, 'but, for my part, once I have eaten this cat and made a hat of his skin, I must die of hunger.'

The cat heard the youngest son saying all this, but he appeared to take no notice of it. Instead, he turned to his master with a grave and serious air and said, 'Do not worry yourself so, my master. All you have to do is give me a bag and get a pair of boots made for me so I may scamper easily through the thorns and brambles, and you shall soon see that, as my owner, you don't have such a poor share after all.'

Although the youngest son did not entirely trust what the cat had said, he remembered that he'd seen the cat play cunning tricks to catch rats and mice. The cat had hung himself by the heels to make the mice think he was dead and had hidden himself in the corn, so the cat's master did not completely despair of the cat helping him out of his situation.

Once his young master had given him his new boots and bag, the cat was very pleased. He thought he looked very gallant and elegant in his shiny boots. Wearing his new boots, the cat hung his bag around his neck and held its strings in his two forepaws. He went out into the fields and found some tender, juicy grass to put in the bag.

Then the cat went to a nearby rabbit warren where he knew a great number of rabbits lived. He stretched himself out on the ground as though he were dead, making sure that some of the grass in the bag was poking out. The cat lay there, waiting for some young rabbits, not yet acquainted with the tricks of the world, to come along and be tempted by the food in his bag.

The cat had barely lain himself down when a young and foolish rabbit hopped up. It sniffed at him, and then climbed into the bag to eat the tender grass. At once, the cat drew closed the strings, catching the rabbit unawares.

Proud of his catch, the cat headed off to the palace and
asked to see the king. He was shown to the king's court, where he
made a low bow to those assembled there.

'I have brought you, Sire, a rabbit from the warren of my
noble lord and master, the Marquis of Carabas (which was the title
that the cat was pleased to invent for his master),' said the cat. 'He
commanded me to bring this to Your Majesty as a gift.'

The king was very pleased with the gift, as he was extremely fond of tasty rabbit.

'Tell thy master,' said the king, 'that I thank him and that I am well pleased with his gift.'

The cat departed, happy with the outcome of his endeavour.

Shortly after this, the cat hid himself amongst some tall corn in a
field, again with his bag around his neck. He stood as still as a statue near
the tastiest-looking corn he could find and held his bag open. It wasn't
long before two partridges came along and, in their efforts to eat the corn,
fell into the open bag. At once, the cat drew the strings closed, catching
both birds.

As he had done with the rabbit, the cat went to the palace and made a present of the partridges to the king. In the same way, the king received the partridges with great pleasure. The king even commanded his servants to reward the cat with a gold coin.

Over the course of the next two or three months, the cat continued to take some of his master's game as a gift to the king. The king was always very pleased to receive these offerings and he always rewarded the cat with a gold coin.

One day, the cat discovered that the king was to go for a drive along the riverside to get some fresh air and enjoy the sunshine. The cat also discovered that the king was taking his daughter, the most beautiful princess in the world, with him on the drive.

The cat went to his master and said, 'If you will follow my advice, your fortune is made. You don't have to do anything apart from going to the river and having a bath at the spot that I show you. Just leave all the rest to me.'

The cat's master was confused as to why the cat was asking him to do this, but he did as the cat advised. While he was bathing, the king's carriage passed by.

At once, the cat cried out at the top of his voice, 'Help! Help! My master, the Marquis of Carabas, is drowning! Help! Help!'

Hearing the noise, the king looked out of the carriage window. Seeing the cat who had brought him so many gifts of game, he commanded his guards to immediately run to the assistance of his Lordship, the Marquis of Carabas.

As the king's guards were pulling the marquis out of the river, the cat hid his master's clothes under a large, heavy rock. Then the cat went up to the coach and told the king that while his master was bathing, some thieves had come and stolen his clothes, even though the cat had cried out, 'Thieves! Thieves!' as loudly as he could. At once, the king commanded some guards to run and fetch one of his best suits for the Marquis of Carabas to wear.

The king was exceedingly polite to the marquis once he had put on the fine suit, as the clothes set off his good looks (for he was very handsome) and the king saw that his lovely daughter was very taken with the marquis. The marquis had only to exchange two or three respectful and tender glances with her before they found themselves in love. The king invited the marquis to join them on their drive.

The cat was overjoyed to see his plan succeeding. He marched on ahead of the coach and met some people mowing in a meadow, which was owned by a cruel ogre.

'Good mowers,' said the cat, 'the ogre who owns this field has asked me to tell you that if you do not tell the king that the meadow you are mowing belongs to the Marquis of Carabas, he will chop you up into tiny pieces and cook you in his pot!'

The mowers were very frightened of the ogre, so when the king drove past and asked them who owned the meadow, they all immediately answered, 'The Marquis of Carabas does, Your Majesty.'

'You have a fine meadow there,' the king said to the marquis.

'Yes Sire,' replied the marquis, thinking quickly. 'It gives me a good harvest every year.'

The cat continued on ahead, until he met with some reapers, who were harvesting corn in another field owned by the ogre.

'Good reapers,' said the cat, 'the ogre who owns this field has asked me to tell you that if you do not tell the king that this corn belongs to the Marquis of Carabas, he will chop you up into tiny pieces and cook you in his pot!'

And when the king passed the field in his carriage and asked them who owned it, they all replied, 'The Marquis of Carabas owns this corn, Your Majesty.'

The cat went on ahead again and told everyone he met that the ogre said to tell the king that the land was owned by the Marquis of Carabas. Everyone was so scared of the ogre that they did.

Eventually the cat came to the ogre's home, which was an enormous, stately castle. The ogre was the richest ogre ever known. The cat, who had discovered the ogre's magical talent, asked to see him, saying he couldn't pass by without paying his respects. After some grumbling, the ogre let him in and made him sit down.

'I have been told that you have an amazing gift,' said the cat to the ogre. 'They tell me that you can change yourself into any creature you choose, such as a lion. Surely this is not true?'

'It is true! If you don't believe me, let me prove it to you,' said the proud ogre, and he turned himself into a fierce, snarling lion.

The cat seemed so terrified at the sight of the lion that he jumped up and tried to climb on to a cupboard, which was rather awkward because of his boots. When he saw the ogre had finally returned to his normal form, he slowly climbed down.

'That is impressive!' said the cat. 'But I have also been told that you can take on the shape of the smallest animal, such as a mouse. Surely, though, that is impossible.'

'Impossible?' roared the ogre. 'Watch and you shall see!'

And the ogre changed himself into a tiny mouse and began to run around the room. The cat immediately sprung on him and ate him up!

Just then, the king's coach drove by the fine castle. The king, wanting to see who lived there, ordered the coach to go in. The cat, hearing the coach coming over the drawbridge, came out to meet them and said to the king, 'Welcome to the castle of my Lord, the Marquis of Carabas!'

'What? My Lord Carabas!' cried the king. 'Does this fine castle belong to you too?

Let us see inside, if you please.'

The marquis helped the princess down from the coach and they followed the king inside the castle. There was a magnificent feast prepared in the Great Hall for the ogre. The king was perfectly charmed with the fine qualities of the marquis, as was the princess, who had fallen completely in love with him.

The king could see that his daughter was in love with the marquis and he was so impressed on seeing the vast estates and fine castle that the marquis owned that he insisted that the marquis and the princess get married that very day.

They lived happily ever after, and the cat became a great lord.
He never had to chase mice again, although he sometimes did for fun!

MONKEYS ON THE BED

Three little monkeys
Jumping on the bed;
One fell off
And knocked his head.
Momma called the doctor,
The doctor said:
'No more monkeys
Jumping on the bed.'

THREE BLIND MICE

Three blind mice, see how they run!
  They all ran after the farmer's wife,
Who cut off their tails with a carving knife;
Did you ever see such a thing in your life,
  As three blind mice?

POP GOES THE WEASEL

Up and down the City Road,
In and out the Eagle,
That's the way the money goes,
Pop goes the weasel!

Half a pound of tuppenny rice,
Half a pound of treacle,
Mix it up and make it nice,
Pop goes the weasel!

Every night when I go out
The monkey's on the table,
Take a stick and knock it off,
Pop goes the weasel!

HEY, DIDDLE, DIDDLE

Hey, diddle, diddle, the cat and the fiddle,
The cow jumped over the moon;
The little dog laughed to see such sport,
And the dish ran away with the spoon.

JACK AND JILL

Jack and Jill went up the hill
To fetch a pail of water;
Jack fell down and broke his crown,
And Jill came tumbling after.

Then up Jack got and home did trot
As fast as he could caper;
He went to bed to mend his head
With vinegar and brown paper.

Goldilocks and the Three Bears

Once upon a time there were three bears who lived together in a house in the woods. One of them was a Father Bear, one was a Mother Bear and the other was a Baby Bear.

They each had a bowl for their porridge: a big bowl for Father Bear, a medium-sized bowl for Mother Bear and a little bowl for Baby Bear. They each had a chair to sit on: a big chair for Father Bear, a medium-sized chair for Mother Bear and a little chair for Baby Bear. And they each had a bed to sleep in: a big bed for Father Bear, a medium-sized bed for Mother Bear and a little bed for Baby Bear.

One day, they made their porridge for breakfast and poured it into the porridge bowls. They decided to go for a walk in the woods while their porridge was cooling so they wouldn't burn their mouths. After all, they were sensible, well-brought-up bears.

While the bears were out walking, a little girl called Goldilocks passed by. She lived on the other side of the woods and had been sent on an errand by her mother. She saw the house and looked in the window. Goldilocks knocked on the door and then bent down and peered in the keyhole. She could see that no one was at home, so she lifted the latch and walked in.

Goldilocks was very pleased when she saw the bowls of porridge sitting on the table. Of course, most people would wait for the bears to come home and hope to be invited to breakfast. However, Goldilocks was rather spoiled and badly brought up, so she set about helping herself.

First she tried Father Bear's porridge, but that was too hot. Next she tried Mother Bear's porridge, but that was too cold. Then she tried Baby Bear's porridge, and that was neither too hot nor too cold. It was just right. Goldilocks liked it so much that she ate it all up.

Then Goldilocks felt tired, so she was pleased when she saw the three chairs. First she tried Father Bear's chair, but that was too hard. Next she tried Mother Bear's chair, but that was too soft. Then she tried Baby Bear's chair, and that was neither too hard nor too soft. It was just right. Goldilocks liked it so much that she sat in it until the chair gave way and she crashed down to the ground. That made her very cross.

Goldilocks was still feeling very tired, so she went upstairs to the bedroom, where she found the three beds. First she tried Father Bear's bed, but that was too hard. Next she tried Mother Bear's bed, but that was too soft. Then she tried Baby Bear's bed, and that was neither too hard nor too soft. It was just right. Goldilocks liked it so much that she pulled the covers over herself and fell fast asleep.

By this time, the three bears thought their porridge would be cool enough and came home to breakfast. When they went to the table, they saw that someone had left the spoons sitting in the porridge.

'Someone has been eating my porridge!' shouted Father Bear.

'Someone has been eating my porridge!' exclaimed Mother Bear.

'Someone has been eating my porridge, and they've eaten it all up!' cried Baby Bear.

The bears realised that somebody had been in their house, so they looked around to see if anything else had been disturbed. When they looked at the chairs, they saw that someone had moved the cushions on the seats around.

'Someone has been sitting in my chair!' shouted Father Bear.

'Someone has been sitting in my chair!' exclaimed Mother Bear.

'Someone has been sitting in my chair, and it's all broken!' cried Baby Bear.

The bears searched further, in case it was a burglar who had been in their house. They went upstairs to their bedroom and saw that the bedclothes on the beds were in disarray.

'Someone has been sleeping in my bed!' shouted Father Bear.

'Someone has been sleeping in my bed!' exclaimed Mother Bear.

'Someone has been sleeping in my bed, and they're still there!' cried Baby Bear.

Goldilocks got a terrible fright when she woke up and saw the three bears standing by the bed, looking at her. She jumped out of the other side of the bed and ran to the open window. She jumped out of the window and landed on the soft, springy grass below. She ran home as fast as she could.

The three bears never saw Goldilocks again, but she learnt her lesson about respecting the belongings of others. And the bears cooked a fresh batch of porridge and had their tasty breakfast!

LITTLE JACK HORNER

*L*ittle Jack Horner
Sat in a corner,
Eating a Christmas pie;
He put in his thumb,
And pulled out a plum,
And said, 'What a good
    boy am I!'

HOT CROSS BUNS

Hot cross buns!
Hot cross buns!
One a penny, two a penny,
Hot cross buns!
If you have no daughters,
Give them to your sons.
One a penny, two a penny,
Hot cross buns!

SIMPLE SIMON

Simple Simon met a pieman,
  Going to the fair;
Said Simple Simon to the pieman,
'Let me taste your ware.'

Said the pieman to Simple Simon,
'Show me first your penny';
Said Simple Simon to the pieman,
'Indeed, I have not any.'

Simple Simon went a-fishing,
For to catch a whale;
All the water he had got
Was in his mother's pail.

Simple Simon went to look
If plums grew on a thistle;
He pricked his fingers very much,
Which made poor Simon whistle

He went for water in a sieve
But soon it all fell through;
And now poor Simple Simon
Bids you all adieu.

POLLY, PUT THE KETTLE ON

Polly, put the kettle on,
  Polly, put the kettle on,
Polly, put the kettle on,
We'll all have tea.

Sukey, take it off again,
Sukey, take it off again,
Sukey, take it off again,
They've all gone away.

I'M A LITTLE TEAPOT

I'm a little teapot, short and stout,
Here is my handle, here is my spout.
When I see the teacups, then I shout,
'Tip me over and pour me out.'

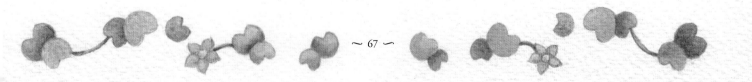

PAT-A-CAKE

Pat-a-cake, pat-a-cake, baker's man,
Bake me a cake as fast as you can;
Pat it and prick it and mark it with B,
Put it in the oven for Baby and me.

Cinderella

Once upon a time there lived a gentleman with his young daughter. His wife had passed away, but their daughter had inherited her mother's rare goodness and sweetness of temper.

After several years had passed, the gentleman decided to marry again. Unhappily, his choice of bride was a poor one, for the lady he married was the proudest and most haughty woman imaginable. She had two daughters of her own, who were like her in every way.

The wedding was barely over when the woman's temper began to show. She could not bear the sweetness of the young girl, as it made her own daughters seem even worse. The stepmother gave her the dirtiest, hardest work in the house to do. Every day, she had to scour the dishes, clean the tables, polish the grates, scrub the floors and dust the bedrooms.

The poor girl was forced to sleep in the cold, bare attic on a pile of straw, while her two stepsisters slept in luxurious beds in fine bedrooms lined with mirrors so they could see their fine clothes. The young girl only had a plain shabby cotton dress to wear.

The girl bore all this patiently and did not even complain to her father, who was completely ruled by his wife, as she did not wish to add to his unhappiness. When her work was done, she would sit in the corner next to the chimney among the cinders. Her stepsisters mocked her and called her 'Cinderella'. However, despite her poor clothes and her daily toil, Cinderella was a hundred times more lovely than her stepsisters, despite their fine clothes.

It came to pass that the king's son came of age. A grand ball was
announced in his honour and the most important and fashionable people
in the town were invited. When their invitation arrived, the stepsisters
immediately busied themselves with choosing their gowns, petticoats and
jewellery for the occasion. Poor Cinderella spent her days lacing corsets,
ironing dresses, picking up discarded clothes, sewing and shopping.
The sisters instructed her to style their hair and paint their faces in
different ways to see what looked best.

On the night of the ball, Cinderella busily dressed the stepsisters. They taunted her, saying, 'Cinderella, don't you wish that you were going to the ball?'

'Ah, you are laughing at me,' Cinderella sighed. 'It is not for such as I to think about going to balls.'

'You are right,' the stepsisters replied. 'How people would laugh to see a cinder wench dancing at a ball!'

With that, the two stepsisters climbed into their fine carriage and drove off to the ball. Cinderella watched until they were out of sight, and then sat in her corner next to the chimney and burst into tears.

Suddenly a kindly little old lady appeared out of nowhere in front of Cinderella, who was so startled that she stopped crying.

'Dear Cinderella, I am your godmother,' said the woman, who was a fairy. 'Why are you crying? Is it because you wish you could go to the ball?'

'Yes, indeed Godmother!' exclaimed Cinderella.

'Well, do what I say and I shall send you there,' said the fairy godmother. 'But first, I must get you ready. Run to the garden and fetch me a pumpkin.'

Cinderella ran out the kitchen door and soon came back with the largest pumpkin she could find. Her fairy godmother laid it on the ground and tapped it with her wand. The simple pumpkin turned into a beautiful coach made of the finest gold.

Next, the fairy godmother looked in the mousetrap in the pantry and saw that six mice were caught there, poking their noses through the bars. As she freed each mouse, the fairy tapped it with her wand. Each mouse turned into a handsome coach horse, with an elegant long neck, a sweeping tail, and a lovely mouse-grey coat.

Then the fairy directed Cinderella to the garden, where she found six lizards. They were soon transformed into six footmen, all wearing shining green and silver coats.

Finally, Cinderella was sent to look in the rat trap. She returned with a great rat with a long beard. One wave of the fairy godmother's wand and the rat turned into a jolly coachman with the finest whiskers imaginable.

'Well my dear, is this equipage fit for the ball?' asked the fairy godmother.

'Why yes!' exclaimed Cinderella. Then she paused and looked down at her shabby, dirty dress. 'But must I go as I am, wearing these rags?'

The fairy godmother touched Cinderella with her wand. Cinderella's shabby dress changed into a beautiful ball gown of gold and silver that sparkled with diamonds. On her feet she wore dainty slippers made of perfect glass.

'Now, my dear, you can go to the ball,' said the fairy godmother. 'Just remember one thing. You must leave before the clock strikes midnight, otherwise your dress will become rags again, your carriage a pumpkin, your horses mice, your footmen lizards and your coachman a rat.'

Cinderella promised she would leave before midnight and then climbed into her coach and drove away, her heart full of joy.

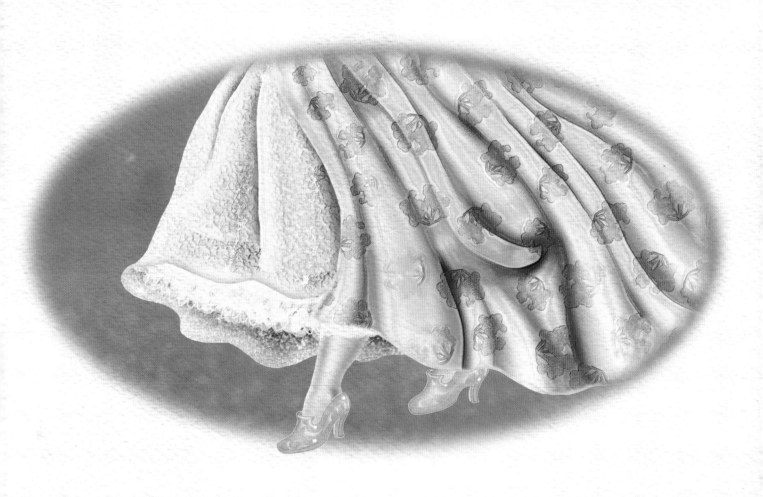

When she arrived at the ball, the whole palace was struck with how beautiful she was. As soon as he saw her, the prince was in love. He came forward and led her into the ballroom and begged her to dance with him the whole evening. Everyone marvelled at her elegance and grace as she danced and all the ladies admired Cinderella's fine gown and imagined how they could have a dress made just like it.

When supper was served, the prince waited on her himself and was so enamoured that he could not eat. Cinderella saw her stepsisters looking at her in admiration, but when she spoke to them, they did not recognise her.

Time passed quickly and soon Cinderella heard the clock chiming eleven and three quarters. She quickly made her exit and returned home.

Cinderella told her fairy godmother about her lovely evening and how the prince had begged her to return for the second night of the ball. As she was talking, she heard her stepsisters return home and ran to meet them, rubbing her eyes as though she had been sleeping.

'If you had been there, you would have seen such a sight!' exclaimed one sister. 'A beautiful princess attended. No one knows who she is but the prince is smitten and would give the world to know her name. How honoured we were when she spoke to us!'

'Oh I would so like to see her,' said Cinderella. 'Could you not lend me a dress so I could attend the ball, just to catch a glimpse?'

'Don't be ridiculous!' snapped the other sister. 'I would not be so silly as to lend my clothes to a cinder maid!' Cinderella was glad, as she had asked in jest and knew that she would be refused.

The next night, the two stepsisters attended the ball and so did
Cinderella, dressed even more magnificently. The prince was constantly
by her side and Cinderella so enjoyed his company that she did not notice
how the time flew by.

Suddenly, Cinderella heard the clock start to strike twelve. She ran from the ballroom as fast as she could. The prince followed but he could not overtake her. As she ran, she left behind one of her glass slippers on the palace stairs. When Cinderella got home, her clothes had returned to rags but she was clutching the other glass slipper.

The stepsisters returned soon after and Cinderella asked them how they had enjoyed the ball and if the mysterious princess had attended. They replied that she had, but when the clock struck twelve, the princess had run from the ballroom in such haste that she had left behind one of her glass slippers. The prince had picked it up and spent the rest of the ball gazing at it, so in love was he.

A few days later, it was proclaimed that the prince would marry whoever could perfectly fit the glass slipper. All the ladies of the court and palace tried on the slipper, but none could fit into it. It was laid upon a silk cushion and taken to all the ladies of the town for them to try, but to no avail.

When it came to the house of the stepsisters, they tried all they could to fit their feet into the slipper. They pushed and shoved and curled their toes, but the slipper was too small and dainty for them.

'Let me try,' said Cinderella.

The two sisters laughed at her and began to tease her, but the courtier who had been sent with the slipper said that he had orders that every woman must try it on. He slipped the slipper on her foot and found that it fitted as perfectly as if it had been made for her.

As the astonished stepsisters looked on, the fairy godmother appeared and waved her wand and they saw before them the beautiful lady from the ball. They threw themselves before Cinderella and begged her to forgive them. Cinderella was so good that she bade them rise and embraced them.

Cinderella was taken to the prince. When he saw her, the prince thought Cinderella was more beautiful than ever and he fell to his knees and asked her to marry him. A few days later they were married and they lived happily ever after.

OLD KING COLE

Old King Cole
Was a merry old soul,
And a merry old soul was he.
He called for his pipe,
And he called for his bowl,
And he called for his fiddlers three.
Every fiddler, he had a fiddle,
And a very fine fiddle had he;
Twee tweedle dee, tweedle dee,
went the fiddlers.
Oh, there's none so rare,
As can compare
With King Cole and his fiddlers three.

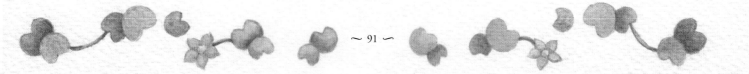

THE GRAND OLD DUKE OF YORK

Oh, the grand old Duke of York,
   He had ten thousand men;
He marched them up to the top of the hill,
And he marched them down again.
And when they were up, they were up,
And when they were down, they were down;
And when they were only halfway up,
They were neither up nor down.

HUMPTY DUMPTY

Humpty Dumpty sat on a wall,
Humpty Dumpty had a great fall;
All the king's horses and all the king's men
Couldn't put Humpty together again.

THERE WAS A CROOKED MAN

There was a crooked man, and he went a crooked mile,
  He found a crooked sixpence against a crooked stile;
He bought a crooked cat, which caught a crooked mouse,
And they all lived together in a little crooked house.

Once upon a time there lived a girl named Little Red Riding Hood. She was called that because she loved to wear a hooded cape of red velvet that her Grandmother had made for her.

One day, her mother said, 'Come Little Red Riding Hood. Your poor Grandmother is ill. I need you to take this bread and cheese to her. Remember, you must stay on the path and go straight there.'

Little Red Riding Hood put the bread and cheese in a basket and set off to her Grandmother's house. Her Grandmother lived on the other side of a nearby wood.

As she was going through the wood, Little Red Riding Hood met a Wolf. The Wolf took one look at Little Red Riding Hood and thought how tasty she looked, but he didn't dare eat her because there were some woodsmen nearby.

'Good day, little maid,' said the Wolf. 'Where are you off to on such a fine day?'

Little Red Riding Hood, who didn't know that it was dangerous to talk to the Wolf, said, 'I am going to see Grandmother. She isn't well, so I am taking her this bread and cheese.'

'Where does she live?' asked the Wolf.

'Why, just through the wood, under the three oak trees,' replied Little Red Riding Hood.

The Wolf thought for a minute, and then said, 'See how pretty the flowers are about here? I am sure your Grandmother would love to see them.'

Little Red Riding Hood looked at the flowers and thought, 'Maybe I should take Grandmother a fresh posy. She'd be so pleased and it is early in the day, so I will still get there in good time.'

'That's a good idea,' said Little Red Riding Hood to the Wolf, and she ran from the path to look for flowers to pick.

Meanwhile, the Wolf ran ahead along the path to Grandmother's house under the three oak trees and knocked on the door.

'Who is there?' asked Grandmother.

'Little Red Riding Hood,' replied the Wolf, imitating her voice, 'with bread and cheese.'

'Come in,' called out Grandmother. 'I am too weak to come to the door.'

The Wolf lifted the latch and went inside. He ate Grandmother in one mouthful. Then he put on a set of her nightclothes and a nightcap, lay down in her bed and drew the curtains so that the room was quite dim.

Little Red Riding Hood gathered a lovely posy of flowers and continued on her way to Grandmother's house. When she got there, she knocked on the door. A husky voice called out, 'Who is there?'

'Little Red Riding Hood, with bread and cheese,' she replied.

'Come in,' called the Wolf. 'I am too weak to come to the door.'

Little Red Riding Hood lifted the latch and went inside. It was quite dark but she could see the shape of her Grandmother under the bedclothes, her nightcap pulled low over her face.

'Put the bread down and come and sit with me,' said the Wolf.

Little Red Riding Hood sat by the bed. She was surprised at how Grandmother looked in her nightclothes.

'Oh Grandmother, what big ears you have!' she said.

'All the better to hear you with,' was the reply.

'Oh Grandmother, what big arms you have!' she said.

'All the better to hug you with,' was the reply.

'Oh Grandmother, what big eyes you have!' she said.

'All the better to see you with,' was the reply.

'Oh Grandmother, what big teeth you have!' she said.

'All the better to eat you with!' was the reply, and the Wolf bounded out of bed and ate Little Red Riding Hood in one mouthful.

The Wolf felt sleepy after his big feast, so he lay down again in the bed and fell asleep. He started to snore very loudly.

Just then, a huntsman who lived nearby was passing the house. 'Goodness, how loudly the old woman is snoring,' he thought. 'She sounds very unwell. I might just pop my head in and see if she is all right.'

The huntsman looked inside and saw the Wolf lying in the bed, fast asleep, his belly full. The huntsman, who had long been hunting the Wolf, took his rifle and was about to shoot when it occurred to him that the Wolf might have eaten the old woman, and she still might be saved.

He took his hunting knife and cut open the Wolf's stomach.
Little Red Riding Hood sprang out, saying, 'Oh, it was so dark in there!'
Then Grandmother slowly climbed out, shaky but alive.

The huntsman went off with the Wolf's skin and Grandmother and
Little Red Riding Hood shared the bread and cheese. 'Never again will
I leave the path to run into the woods when my mother has forbidden it,'
Little Red Riding Hood thought to herself as she finished her delicious food.

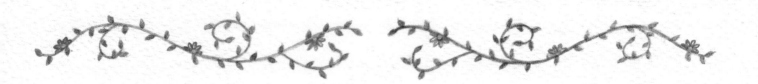

ONE, TWO, THREE, FOUR, FIVE

One, two, three, four, five,
　　Once I caught a fish alive;
Six, seven, eight, nine, ten,
Then I let it go again.

Why did you let it go?
Because it bit my finger so.
Which finger did it bite?
This little finger on the right.

SING A SONG OF SIXPENCE

Sing a song of sixpence,
A pocket full of rye;
Four and twenty blackbirds
Baked in a pie.

When the pie was opened
The birds began to sing;
Wasn't that a dainty dish
To set before the king?

The king was in his counting-house
Counting out his money;
The queen was in the parlour
Eating bread and honey.

The maid was in the garden
Hanging out the clothes,
When down came a blackbird,
And pecked off her nose.

RYE

FIVE LITTLE DUCKS

Five little ducks went out one day
  Over the hills and far away.
Mother duck said, 'Quack quack, quack quack!'
But only four little ducks came back.

Four little ducks went out one day
Over the hills and far away.
Mother duck said, 'Quack quack, quack quack!'
But only three little ducks came back.

Three little ducks went out one day
Over the hills and far away.
Mother duck said, 'Quack quack, quack quack!'
But only two little ducks came back.

Two little ducks went out one day
Over the hills and far away.
Mother duck said, 'Quack quack, quack quack!'
But only one little duck came back.

One little duck went out one day
Over the hills and far away.
Mother duck said, 'Quack quack, quack quack!'
But none of those five little ducks came back.

Mother duck she went out one day
Over the hills and far away.
Mother duck said, 'Quack quack, quack quack!'
And all of those five little ducks came back.

THREE LITTLE KITTENS

Three little kittens, they lost their mittens,
And they began to cry;
Oh, mother dear, we sadly fear
That we have lost our mittens.
What! Lost your mittens, you naughty kittens!
Then you shall have no pie.
Mee-ow, mee-ow, mee-ow,
No, you shall have no pie.

Three little kittens, they found their mittens,
And they began to cry;
Oh, mother dear, see here, see here,
For we have found our mittens.
Put on your mittens, you silly kittens,
And you shall have some pie.
Purr-r, purr-r, purr-r,
Oh, let us have some pie.

Three little kittens put on their mittens,
And soon ate up the pie;
Oh, mother dear, we greatly fear
That we have soiled our mittens.
What! Soiled your mittens,
    you naughty kittens!
Then they began to sigh,
Mee-ow, mee-ow, mee-ow,
Then they began to sigh.

The three little kittens, they washed their mittens,
And hung them out to dry;
Oh, mother dear, do you not hear
That we have washed our mittens?
What! Washed your mittens, you good little kittens,
But I smell a rat close by.
Mee-ow, mee-ow, mee-ow,
We smell a rat close by.

INCY WINCY SPIDER

*I*ncy Wincy Spider
Climbed up the water spout.
Down came the rain
And washed poor Incy out.

Out came the sunshine
And dried up all the rain,
And Incy Wincy Spider
Climbed up the spout again.

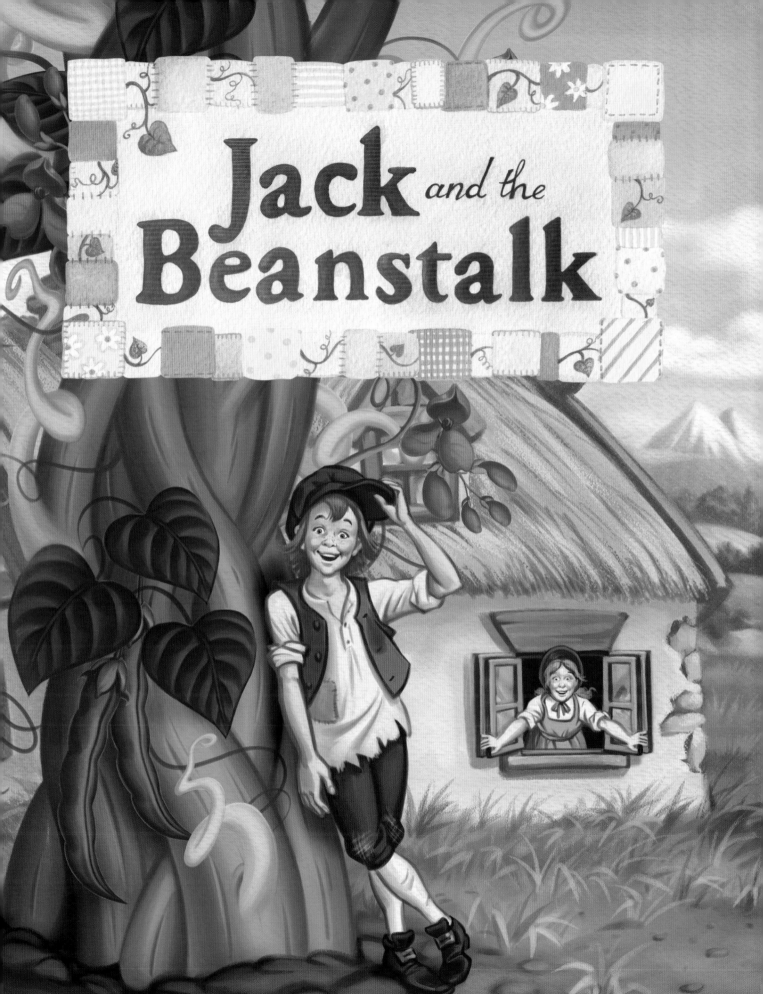

Jack and the Beanstalk

Once upon a time there lived a poor widow in a little cottage with her only son Jack. They were very poor. Jack had no work, so all they had to live on was the milk given by their cow, Milky-White, which they took to market each morning and sold. Jack was a kind-hearted and quick boy, but he was also giddy and wilful.

Then one day, Milky-White stopped giving milk. After several days of this, Jack's mother said to him, 'We must sell Milky-White at the market and use the money to start a shop or something.'

'All right Mother,' said Jack. 'Today is market day. I'll soon sell Milky-White and then we'll see what we can do with the money. I'll make sure I get the best price I can.'

So Jack took Milky-White's rope and set off down the road with her to town. As he walked along, he met a funny-looking old man who stopped and said to him, 'Hello Jack! Where are you off to?'

'Good morning,' replied Jack, wondering all the while how this strange fellow knew his name. 'I'm off to market to sell our cow.'

The man stretched out his hand and showed Jack five curious beans. They were all sorts of colours and shimmered and shone. 'These beans are of great value. I'd be prepared to do a swap with you – your cow for my beans.'

'You don't say,' said Jack. He agreed to the sale and handed over Milky-White's rope.

Jack headed home again, the five beans in his pocket. His mother was surprised to see him home so soon.

'Back already Jack?' she asked. 'How much did you sell Milky-White for? What, five pounds? Ten? Fifteen? Surely not twenty!'

'What about these?' said Jack, and he stretched out his hands to show her the beans. His mother took them and looked at them.

'What!' she exclaimed. 'Have you been such a fool as to give away my Milky-White for a handful of beans? What shall we do? How could you? As for these beans, out the window they go!'

Jack's angry mother threw the beans out the window and sent him to bed without any supper. He was very sad and sorry, not just for the missed supper but for his mother's sake as well. It was several hours before he fell asleep.

When Jack woke up the next morning, his room seemed different. Normally bright and sunny, it was strangely dark and shady. He ran to his window and looked out. To his amazement, he saw that the beans had grown in the night. They had formed a beanstalk that climbed up and up until it vanished into the clouds. Jack ran down to the garden to take a closer look.

'Why, those beans have twined together so that you could climb it
like a ladder,' thought Jack. 'I wonder where it ends.'

Jack began to climb the beanstalk. It bore his weight easily.
He climbed until everything below him – his house, the road, the town –
all began to look quite small. He climbed and he climbed and he climbed
until he was quite tired. He stopped to rest for a short while, and then he
continued on.

Finally, Jack reached the top of the beanstalk. He found himself next to a long straight road that ran through some lovely countryside of woods, pastures and a crystal clear stream burbling along. In the far distance along the road stood a great castle of stone.

Jack set off along the road towards the castle. He walked and walked until he came to the stone castle. Standing on the doorstep was a big, tall woman. She was a giant.

'Good morning ma'am,' said Jack politely. 'Would you be so kind as to give me some breakfast?' Jack was as hungry as a hunter, as he was sent to bed without his supper.

'It's breakfast you want, is it?' said the woman. 'It's breakfast you'll be if you don't get along. My man is a giant and there's nothing he likes better than a boy for breakfast! He'll be here soon. Move along or I'll cook you myself!'

'Oh please ma'am, don't cook me,' said Jack. 'I'd be willing to serve you if you'd be so good as to hide me from your husband and give me some breakfast.'

'There's a good boy,' said the giantess, very pleased with the idea of a boy to help her. She took Jack into the kitchen and gave him a hunk of bread and cheese and some milk.

As Jack was finishing his breakfast, the whole house started to shake. Jack heard a loud noise in the distance, getting closer. Thump! Thump! Thump!

'It's my husband!' exclaimed the giantess. 'Quick, hide in here!'
She bundled Jack into the oven and shut the door just as the giant came in.

The giant was enormous. He had been out hunting and had three calves hanging from his belt. 'Cook me a couple of these for my breakfast!' he bellowed and flung them on the table. Then the giant paused, sniffed the air and cried out in a voice like thunder:

'Fee-fi-fo-fum,
I smell the blood of an Englishman!
Be he alive or be he dead,
I'll grind his bones to make my bread.'

Then he shouted, 'There is a man in the castle! Let me have him for my breakfast!'

'Nonsense,' said the giantess. 'You've grown old and silly! It must be the man you had for dinner yesterday. Go and wash up and I'll have your breakfast ready for you.'

The giant left to wash up and Jack opened the oven door to jump out, but the giantess told him to wait. 'He will have a sleep after breakfast and then you can come out,' she said.

The giantess cooked two of the calves for the giant's breakfast which he wolfed down hungrily. Then the giant went to a big chest and took out some bags of gold. He sat down and began to count out the money, until eventually his head began to nod and he started to snore so loudly that the house shook.

Jack crept out of the oven. As he went past the giant, he took one of the bags of gold and then ran as fast as he could to the beanstalk. He threw down the gold and climbed down after it. When he got home, he showed his mother the bag of gold and said, 'See mother? Wasn't I right to buy those beans? They are magical!'

Jack and his mother lived off the gold for some time, but at last it ran out. He decided to try his luck at the top of the beanstalk again. Jack climbed and he climbed until he reached the top. When he came to the castle, the giantess was again standing on the doorstep.

'Good morning,' said Jack. 'Could you give me some breakfast?'

The giantess looked at him suspiciously, unsure if she knew him. 'Go away boy,' she said, 'or my husband will eat you for breakfast. But wait, are you the youngster who came here before? My husband lost a bag of gold that day.'

'That's strange ma'am,' said Jack. 'I dare say I could tell you something about that but I'm so hungry that I couldn't speak until I had some breakfast.'

The giantess was curious, so she took Jack in and gave him some breakfast. As he was finishing, Jack heard a loud thumping in the distance and the house began to shake. 'Quick, into the oven!' exclaimed the giantess, and Jack scrambled in. The giant bellowed:

'Fee-fi-fo-fum,
I smell the blood of an Englishman!
Be he alive or be he dead,
I'll grind his bones to make my bread.'

The giantess scolded him and the giant had his breakfast. Then he said, 'Wife, bring me my hen that lays the gold eggs.'

The giantess brought in the hen and the giant said, 'Lay!' The hen laid an egg made entirely of gold. After a while, the giant's head began to nod and he started to snore so loudly that the house shook.

Jack crept out of the oven, grabbed hold of the hen and ran for all he was worth. As he ran, the hen cackled and Jack heard the giant wake up and call out, 'Wife, wife, what have you done with the hen?'

That was all Jack heard before he rushed down the beanstalk. When he got home, he showed his mother the hen and said 'Lay' to it. It laid a golden egg every time he told it to.

Still, Jack was not content and decided to try his luck up the beanstalk again. He climbed and he climbed until he reached the top but this time he did not walk along the road to the house.

Jack crept along and hid behind a bush until he saw the giantess come out to the well. Then he slipped into the house and climbed into a large copper boiler. He hadn't been there long before he heard a loud thumping noise and the giant and his wife came into the kitchen.

The giant sniffed and then bellowed:

'Fee-fi-fo-fum,

I smell the blood of an Englishman!

Be he alive or be he dead,

I'll grind his bones to make my bread.'

'Do you?' asked the giantess. 'If it's that little rogue who stole your gold and your hen, he's bound to be in the oven.'

Luckily, Jack had not hidden there, and the giantess said, 'Well, there you go again with your fee-fi-fo-fum! It must be that man we ate last night that you can smell.'

The giant sat down to breakfast, but throughout the meal he kept muttering 'I could swear...' to himself and he would get up and look in the larder and the cupboards. Luckily, he did not think of the copper boiler. After breakfast, the giant said, 'Wife, bring me my golden harp.'

The giantess put the harp on the table in front of him and the giant said, 'Sing!' At once, the golden harp began to sing most beautifully. It sang until the giant's head began to nod and he started to snore so loudly that the house shook.

Then Jack quietly lifted the lid of the boiler and climbed out.
He crept up to the table and grabbed hold of the golden harp and dashed
to the door.

But the magic harp called out, 'Master! Master!' in a loud voice,
and the giant woke to see Jack running out the door.

Jack ran as fast as he could but the giant ran faster. He had nearly
caught Jack when they reached the beanstalk and Jack dodged and
then disappeared into the ground. The giant looked down and saw Jack
climbing down for dear life.

For a minute, the giant hesitated and then he swung himself down on to the beanstalk. It swayed and shook with the giant's weight as he made his way down.

Jack climbed faster and faster until he was nearly home. Then he called out, 'Mother! Mother! Bring the axe! Bring the axe!'

Jack's mother came rushing out with the axe in her hand, but stopped in fright when she saw the giant making his way down the beanstalk. Jack jumped down and grabbed the axe and chopped at the mighty beanstalk until it was cut in two.

The beanstalk began to topple and fall, and the terrible giant fell down with it and lay still, never to eat anyone again.

By selling the golden eggs and showing the golden harp, Jack and his mother became very rich. Jack married a great princess and they all lived happily ever after, but they never knew what became of the funny-looking old man who sold Jack the beans.

ROW, ROW, ROW YOUR BOAT

Row, row, row your boat,
Gently down the stream,
Merrily, merrily, merrily, merrily,
Life is but a dream.

A SAILOR WENT TO SEA, SEA, SEA

A sailor went to sea, sea, sea,
To see what he could see, see, see;
But all that he could see, see, see,
Was the bottom of the deep
  blue sea, sea, sea!

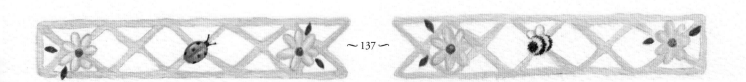

WEE WILLIE WINKIE

Willie Winkie runs through the town,
  Upstairs and downstairs in his nightgown,
Rapping at the window, crying through the lock,
'Are all the children in their beds,
  It's past eight o'clock!'

ROCK-A-BYE, BABY, ON THE TREE TOP

Rock-a-bye, baby, on the tree top,
When the wind blows, the cradle will rock;
When the bough breaks, the cradle will fall,
Down will come baby, cradle and all.

ROCK-A-BYE, BABY, THY CRADLE IS GREEN

Rock-a-bye, baby, thy cradle is green,
Father's a nobleman, Mother's a queen.
And Betty's a lady and wears a gold ring,
And Johnny's a drummer and drums for the king.

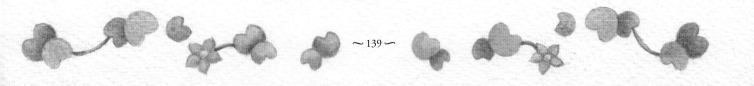

TWINKLE, TWINKLE, LITTLE STAR

Twinkle, twinkle, little star,
How I wonder what you are!
Up above the world so high,
Like a diamond in the sky.

When the blazing sun is gone,
When he nothing shines upon,
Then you show your little light,
Twinkle, twinkle all the night.

Then the traveller in the dark,
Thanks you for your tiny spark,
He could not see which way to go,
If you did not twinkle so.

In the dark blue sky you keep,
And often through my curtains peep,
Do you never shut your eye
Till the sun is in the sky.

As your bright and tiny spark
Lights the traveller in the dark,
Though I know not what you are,
Twinkle, twinkle little star.

STAR WISH

Star light, star bright,
First star I see tonight,
I wish I may, I wish I might,
Have the wish I wish tonight.

AND SO GOODNIGHT!

Here's a body – there's a bed!
There's a pillow – here's a head!
There's a curtain – here's a light!
There's a puff – and so goodnight!

The End